Oddball Opposites!

Nathalie Butler

PowerKiDS press

New York

Published in 2018 by The Rosen Publishing Group, Inc.
29 East 21st Street, New York, NY 10010

First Edition

Book Design: Brian Garvey
Illustrations by Continuum Content Solutions

Cataloging-in-Publication Data
Names: Butler, Nathalie.
Title: Oddball opposites / Nathalie Butler.
Description: New York : PowerKids Press, 2018. | Series: Learning with stories
| Includes index.
Identifiers: ISBN 9781508162377 (pbk.) | ISBN 9781508162391 (library
bound) | ISBN 9781508162384 (6 pack) | ISBN 9781508162407 (ebook)
Subjects: LCSH: English language–Synonyms and antonyms–Juvenile
fiction.
Classification: LCC PZ7.O333 2018 | DDC [E]–dc23

CPSIA Compliance Information: Batch #BS17PK: For further information contact Rosen Publishing, New York, New York

at 1-800-237-9932

Manufactured in the United States of America

Contents

Let's take a trip to Monster Town!

This town is filled with opposites.

How many can be found?

One monster is up
and the other is down.

Which monster is which in Monster Town?

The red monster is big.

He bumps his head!

The pink monster is small.

That must hurt!

she said.

9

One monster is far
and the other is near.

Near and far are opposites,
that should be clear.

The blue monster is fast.

The yellow monster is slow.

Hurry up, slowpoke.

We've got a long way to go!

One monster is quiet,
the other is loud.

Which one will never get lost in a crowd?

The pink monster is first.
That makes her glad.

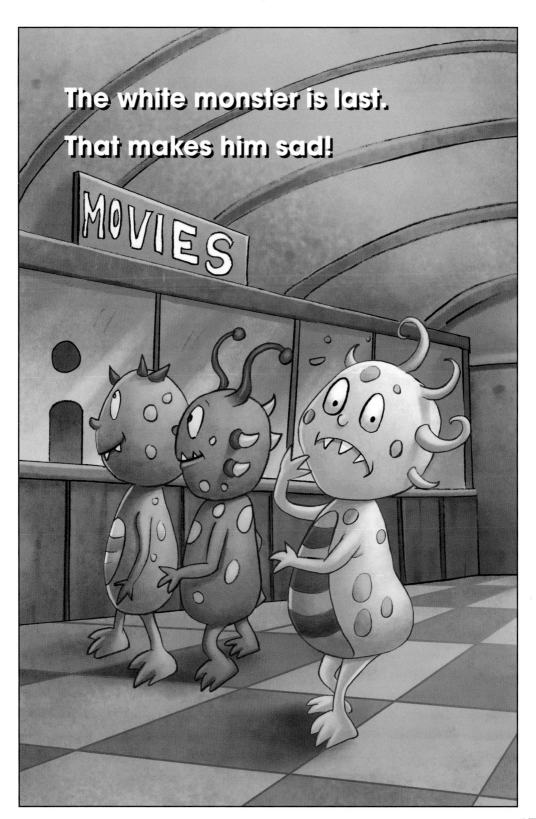

The white monster is last.
That makes him sad!

The brown monster is messy.

The orange monster is neat.

Come on, brown monster,
please wash your feet!

The fiery monster is hot.

The drippy monster is cold.

The red monster is young.

The blue monster is old.

Monster Town is a great place to go.

Now you know it's true.

The monsters know a lot
about opposites.

And now you do too!

Words to Know

drippy

fiery

sad

Index